First published in 2008 by Simply Read Books
www.simplyreadbooks.com

Text copyright © 2008 Eleri Glass
Illustrations copyright © Ashley Spires

Cataloguing in Publication Data
Glass, Eleri, 1969-
        The red shoes / by Eleri Glass ; illustrated by Ashley Spires.
ISBN 978-1-894965-78-1
        I. Spires, Ashley, 1978- II. Title.
PS8613.L383R43 2008   jC813'.6   C2007-905127-8

We gratefully acknowledge the support of the Canada Council for the Arts and
the BC Arts Council for our publishing program.

Printed in Singapore

10 9 8 7 6 5 4 3 2 1

Book design by Robin Mitchell-Cranfield for hundreds & thousands

the red shoes

ELERI GLASS *with illustrations by* ASHLEY SPIRES

My feet huff, puff
like two tired trains.

So many shoes
squatting on the shelves,
white and brown, lace-ups
and boots.

My eyes hunt,
my toes tingle.
They call me from the corner,
ruby whispers,
shiny silver giggles.

I slip my hands inside
and walk them across the shelf.
Sing a tiny shoe tune.

Mom picks up the lace-ups.
I pull on her hand.
"The red ones, Mom."

The shoe lady measures my feet
with the metal monster.
Boy, have they grown
since last time!

Four pairs, in white, in brown,
lined up beside me.
The shoe lady criss-crosses
the laces,
pulls them tight.

"Walk around the room."
I scuff a brown, lace-up circle,
heading for the red ones.

Mom tests the toes.
Too big, too small.
Two tired feet,
four empty boxes,
eight cranky shoes.

The red shoes are happy apples,
waiting to be picked.
"The red ones, Mom."

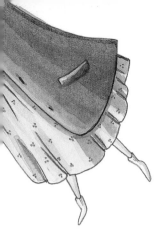

Here comes the shoe lady,
box in hand.

One red shoe
swings high, just out of reach.

Slide my feet inside them.
Cherry blossom sweet
the breeze that lifts me
off my feet.

Down I come, before my mom,
skirt drawn up, so we can see.
"The red ones, Mom."

"Thank you, Mom."

Take them from the box,
white paper so thin it shines.

Mom comes to tuck me in.
She laughs when I pull the sheets
tight against my chin.
"What are you hiding?"
She kisses me on the forehead.

The red shoes giggle,
as I fall asleep.

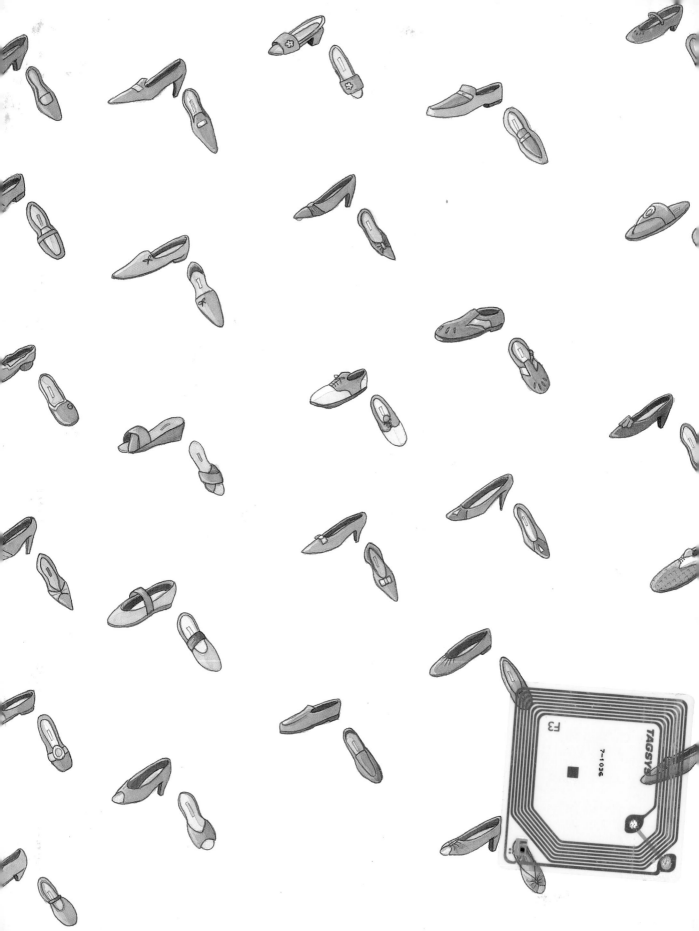